Fruits and Finery

Short Stories of Horror, Myth, and Legend
By Cat Webling

Table of Contents

Dedicated to the lives I've lived that line my shelves, the ones we tell each other when we need to escape.

Introduction

I like to think that all of my short stories have some kind of theme to them. I write a lot of fantasy and science fiction, mostly because that takes up the majority of what I read, but I also like to throw in the occasional horror story. What can I say? I have a macabre imagination. So, it's not necessarily the genre that connects my work.

No, I think it's more that I really like to write about human (or other) nature. I like writing about things that make your skin crawl or your heart sing, or leave you questioning what you know about the world around you without giving you any superficial answers about it. If you come away from my stories thinking about anything at all, I'm happy.

This collection is a little different from my last one. *The Clockwork Figurine* was a collection of snippets inspired by a ton of wildly different things, thrown together a little randomly. This collection, though, has a bit more structure; I set out to write a bunch of beginnings. Each of these stories has the potential to be more in their own right, but deserve to be seen for what they are when they stand alone. "The Graveyard," for instance, reads like to prologue to an epic fantasy novel. Who knows? Someday it might be. I just really liked the idea of a girl meeting a dragon when they should have been extinct.

I think that's another theme of this collection: meeting the unknown. I don't want to cast that as particularly positive or negative; in every story, someone meets something completely unknown. What they do from there is up to them. I just like the idea of the impossible, and proving that it's not really as infallible as it looks. In a year that was too full of the impossible being dreadful, I wanted to write about impossibles that didn't have to be.

Here's hoping your impossibles are as nice as some of these, and not as dark as others.

Happy reading,

Cat

The Graveyard

The small girl pulled her bedraggled, but still fine, shawl closer around her, glad when the echoes of her footsteps no longer came back to her from the depths of the valley. She stood before ancient pillars that curled toward the sky as if they'd been carved from the earth itself and stripped of all color, drained by the eons they had seen, stretching out in solemn pairs of guards as far as she could see.

On the ground not far from her was what looked to be a broken piece of one of the columns. Kneeling to get a better look, she could see the scratches and nicks that centuries of use had imparted on it. She hovered, not quite daring to touch for a long moment, as if what this might have been could still rise up and swallow her whole. Finally, with some force of will, her hand settled on the worn surface. It was colder than she'd been expecting, like touching a river stone in the early spring. Rough, but not uninviting.

Something crackled behind her, making her jump nearly out of her skin and turn on her heel, hands up before her with palms flat out. This might have looked like a frightened plea for mercy if not for the hard-eyed grimace set on her face.

Nothing should still be here. Nothing at all should have been here for centuries. There was no way anything could be here.

"You have tread where none should come."

She couldn't move.

The pounding of its feet shook the very stone beneath her feet, not like the fall of boulders in the mountain pass that she had narrowly avoided to arrive here, but like the rumble of the ground when the gods shook the world, or when armies of soldiers on horseback passed by on the horizon. It was a subtle power that spoke of something so much more.

"Tell me, little one," the silken voice said, with some hint of amusement, "why have you come to disturb my family's bones?"

"I-" She choked on her words. The air seemed to tingle with a strange power, stinging her skin. She swallowed, and started again. "I mean you no harm...no offense, at all. I...I came only seeking..."

"Seeking?" The amusement grew sharp. "Do you seek the tooth you dared to violate with your touch? The properties your legends imbue it with?"

The cold shape at her feet seemed to be calling to her, but she did not spare a glance for it, eyes still locked into the darkness they could not penetrate.

"I seek assistance," she said, voice wavering but not yet breaking.

The rumbling, which had paused briefly with the voice's questioning, began again, shifting off to her left to come before her, and yet she could still see nothing. She seemed to have its attention, at the very least. "That is...different. Why would you come to this empty place for assistance?"

"I had nowhere else to turn." She blinked rapidly against the burning in her eyes, and again, her voice wavered unsteadily. "Please. They're dying."

"And well they should. Poachers. Desecrators. Thieves and vandals." There was no malice still in the voice, though the silk of it was turning slowly to stone with her every breath. It said the words as if they were facts, with all the certainty of one who had seen these things first hand.

"We have not seen your kind for an age. My people are innocents, they do not deserve to die."

"Do they not? They live on the backs of my slaughtered race." The stone seemed settled in the voice, and the calm of it seemed more forced to her ears. "Why should I help you, when you will take your knowledge of my survival back to your little village, and bring them back to hunt me down for my scales or my blood or my own bones?"

"No."

There was a pause, and some of the silken interest returned. "No?"

"Some would. I will not."

The rumbling grew slightly closer, and from the furthest edge of the low light still spilling into the valley from the setting sun, sulfurous breath swept over her face like a gust of hot wind. "And why is that, little one?"

"Will you allow me to see you before I give you my reasons?"

There was a long pause, then something that might have been a laugh echoed toward her. "Very well."

The creature that stepped into the light before her might have been made of cast gold. The scales glittered iridescently even in the dimness, shimmering every time it drew breath. It towered over her, looming like the façade of the Baron's manor if it were twice its size. How it spoke with the jaw of jagged teeth, longer than greatswords, she could not tell. Smoke rose from its nostrils, as if it were already deciding how she would taste well charred, and its eyes...its eyes were fascinating. They oscillated between deepest honey brown and glowing coals, and seemed almost to draw her in as they focused down on her face, sparkling with an intelligence that spoke of a lifetime of knowledge and a newfound curiosity.

The perpetual grin of its mouth opened. "Tell me."

She stood as straight as she could manage, took a deep breath, and spoke. "I have heard the tales of the days when your kind were free to roam, and dwelled among my ancestors. They speak of raids on your lairs filled with our precious stones, stolen from the bodies of soldiers who came before them, and of burning villages whose smoke filled your wings and whose livestock filled your bellies. They speak of the terrible dangers of your kind, the cruelty and the mockery and the soul-deep evil that dwells in all of you...but I don't see it."

The creature tilted its head and nearly seemed to smile. "And why is that?"

She took a shaky step toward him. "I see a race that sought to protect their homes. I see a race beset by mine, who would attack each other for petty differences and squabble over power when food has run scarce. I see creatures searching for food and being struck down for not understanding the concept of an owned field or herd. I see that you have done no wrong by your standard, and we have failed to see what those standards are and explain our own before we acted, and now, when we ruin each other for titles and land, we have no one to turn to, to save us from ourselves."

"You wish that I should save you?"

"I wish that you should help me save them."

A long moment of silence passed, and just before she lost all courage she may have had, it spoke again.

"What would you ask of me?"

"Help me protect my home, and I will ensure that they cannot ever hurt you again."

"How would you propose to do that? You are small and weak."

Finally, she smiled, and felt her eyes light up with the familiar forest green glow that she had come to love. "I am not as they are. Blessed, or cursed, I do not know, but I do know that I am feared. This time, it will be of use."

Sometimes It's Quiet

The end of the world didn't look anything like we thought it was going to.

There were no fires. There was no screaming in the streets...well, not at first. No gunshots were aimed at brick fronts that were full of armies of the unruly dead, or aliens that'd for some reason decided that humanity was to be systematically eliminated. It had nothing to do with corrupted world leaders starting nuclear Armageddon over something ridiculous, although it got really close to that a few times in the lead-up. No, it was nothing like any of those books I used to like to read back before it happened.

The end of the world was...quiet.

One day, I woke up to find that the rest of the world wasn't there to do the same. They were just gone, and there was no reason for it. Tellies were left on some show they never finished, washing was left half out on the line, cars rolled to a stop where they were. There were no wars or riots or all that because there weren't enough people left for there to be.

I woke up, and the rest of the world was silent.

Of course, that doesn't really mean there was no panicking. I panicked, and I proper panicked. I woke up, and Mum and Dad were just gone. Mum didn't call up the stairs like she always did, telling me to hurry up or I'll be late, again. Dad wasn't singing off-key '80's music in the shower down the hall. Juno was still locked in his cage, whining because he was hungry or because he needed a wee horribly, I couldn't tell. Normally he'd have been licking my face, all covered in grass stains, and Mum would have to pull him off me with a huff about "messy little whatsit." That day, his whines were the only sound in the whole house.

I spent all morning running down the high street, screaming for them, for someone, anyone to answer me. No one did.

You learn to live with it after a while. The quiet, the pain, the sadness. They come in waves, crashing like a tsunami until you can't breathe anymore, and you can't see the surface because you've been sucked in too far. Eventually, though, when you've cried as hard as you can for as long as your body will let you, you stand back up and you move on. There's work to be done.

My first stop in the morning is usually Mrs. McCready's, to pick up the milk and Juno's food. He's getting big, and I can't carry the huge bags into the house on my own yet, so I pick him up a little packet of food for the day and occasionally a treat from the big glass jar on the counter, calmly telling the empty air that I'll pay my tab off when there's someone to pay.

The treats are running low now, and I don't know where she keeps them to refill it. He'll be sad when they're gone, and so will I.

From there, I walk up the path to my back garden, and let myself in through the kitchen. There's Juno, barking in the window again. Mum'll be upset that he's getting up on the counters. He was too little to reach before, and it's getting harder to shove him down off the counter again every time I come home. I make my breakfast and take him out for a walk, always on a lead unless we're going to the beach. It's only polite, wouldn't want him rooting through the neighbor's gardens. After that, I'll haul out Dad's lawnmower and get to work trimming the place up. If not that, then I'll sweep up in Mrs. McCready's or the church, or I'll pick up litter from the side of the highway on the edge of town, providing I can ride my bike all the way out there. I don't do that as often anymore. There isn't much litter left around here. That's a nice side effect, I guess.

When I'm tired, and if I'm particularly put out, I'll sneak into the Awl and Grindstone. I've always looked at the taps behind the counter, but I still haven't tried any of them. Jim the Barman always said it just tasted like gone-off bread, but I think he was telling me that so I wouldn't try to take any. I suppose I might be able to have some now, I think I'm old enough. I don't really know. I don't guess that it matters much either way. Then it's home again, and I'll take Juno out for another walk. Sometimes I'll just play with him in the yard, or when it's cold, I'll stoke up a fire. Dad taught me how ages ago but I used to not be allowed near the matches. It gets really cold without a heater working, though, so I don't think he'd mind. Anyway, I get to make cheese toasties when I do that, which was fun for a while.

We usually fall asleep in the den. Juno doesn't fit in his crate anymore, and I don't like being up in my room.

There's always a part of me that hopes that when I wake up, Mum and Dad will be frowning at me and asking how I've gotten so bloody tall, and why I kipped on the couch when I have my own perfectly good bed upstairs. There's always a part of me that knows that someday, I might just not wake up at all, and finally find out where everyone else has gone. The rest of me knows that probably, I'll wake up, and I'll take Juno for a walk, and I'll go to Mrs. McCready's for the milk. Sometimes, I know which one I'm hoping for the most. Sometimes, I don't know if I'm hoping for anything at all.

Sometimes, it's quiet.

What Lies Beyond

Heaven is a very strange idea. We dream that one day, when we're old and fulfilled, we'll take our final breath, close our eyes, and end up somewhere where we'll be rewarded for everything we've ever done right. Every smile at a passing stranger and quarter in a hobo's tin is a token you can redeem in the Hereafter. We dream that only good people end up there, and we know exactly how we'll be judged, what to avoid, what to do and say to guarantee our spot. We dream that we're all good people.

But there's a funny thing about Heaven. We all seem to know what we'll be getting, but we can't seem to agree on what it'll look like when we get there. Oh, I'm sure that there's a good many people that imagine bright, shining gates, glittering with gold or pearls. Maybe they think of thick, fluffy, white clouds that go on forever. Maybe they think that you're personally greeted by Saint Peter, with his long scroll of a list in hand as he reads you your rights and tells you your fate. Maybe they think they'll be greeted by the people who loved you and left you too soon, warm smiles and warm words that pull you into the eternal embrace. Maybe you just show up in a plain white void, and are content to stay there, not having to think about anything ever again. I can see why that would appeal.

Yes, everyone seems to have a rough guess as to what we'll see when we get past the end, but the funniest part to me? We don't tend to imagine the way up to Heaven. We don't imagine that we'll have to travel there; most folks just assume they'll arrive immediately. Of all the religious texts and mythos and beliefs, there's very few in the world that imagine what you'll see immediately before you get there. From all I've seen, most people never assumed that they'd need to catch a lift upwards.

One minute, I was standing on the front lines somewhere in a country that felt like it was impossibly far from where I grew up, with the scraps of the letters I'd been reading that morning clutched as close to the trigger as I could hold them, rustling as I looked down the sights and waited like a fool for them to be close enough to hit, and watching with a lump in my throat as one of them lifted their gun, and I couldn't seem to shoot, why couldn't I shoot, I need to shoot, I need-

And then next, I was walking through Grand Central, dressed to the nines as if I were just going down to the office.

I was pretty certain I wasn't going to be late. Besides, my officemate Jim was always in at ten past eight anyway with a couple of donuts if he could snag them from the bakery up the street. I always left in plenty of time, and though there were no clocks, I noticed dreamily, but it didn't matter. I'd never been late, except for...when the draft came up.

But if the draft came up, why was I...?

I looked down, perplexed to find myself in my favorite faux-Italian suit. It'd always looked more expensive than it felt, and fit better than a hand-me-down had any right to. It was my favorite because it was the only suit I could afford, but Jim had always said it made me look like a Wall Street mogul. The only problem was that I hadn't worn this suit in three years. I hadn't worn anything but my uniform in three years, and I hadn't seen the office since the radio had called the dates and mine had been the last on the list.

"Looking for the train, honey?"

I looked up to see a kindly old woman standing beside me. I hadn't heard her come up, but for some reason, I wasn't startled. She smiled at me genially and motioned for me to walk with her. Still stunned, I did.

"Uh...I s'pose I am, but where...?"

"You got your passport?"

I frowned. You didn't need a passport for a train. But the woman nodded at my hand, and I noticed for the first time that I had a little book in it. It was about the size of a sketchbook that you might see a kid carrying to school in their bag, with old black leather for the cover and pages that looked used, as if they didn't quite fit together anymore with the ink soaked into them. She held out her hand for it and I gave it to her numbly, watching as she calmly flicked it open and started thumbing through it.

"Uh, ma'am, I don't want to be rude, but where are we?"

She smiled, but didn't look up from her reading. "We're in the terminal." Helpful.

"Which terminal? Going where? How did I get here? I should have been-"

"You're a soldier?"

I blinked. "I...yes, I am. Or I was. How did you-?"

She tapped the page in front of her, still not looking up. "Says you were reserves for a while, and ended up on the front lines pretty late."

"Yes. Yes, that's true, but how do you know that? What's that book?"

"Your passport," she repeated, flipping to the next page. Apparently, something was written there that she wasn't expecting, and she finally looked up at me. "You never fired?"

"What?"

"Your gun, honey, you never fired it?"

I'm sure I colored a little bit. "Well, I fired it in training. I was a damn fine shot. They always said I was damn good for a city kid. But...no...not *at* anyone, no. I don't know why that's significant." I didn't know why I was telling her any of this to begin with, or how she knew. What was that book? I reached for it. "Can I see that please?"

She held it back from me. "Oh no, honey, that's against procedure. You know how they are about rules."

"They?" But she wouldn't elaborate.

Seeing as she didn't seem to want to help me, I looked around for some clues as to what was going on. The platform we were walking down looked exactly like it might have been Grand Central, except for the fact that the big windows way overhead seemed to look out on to nothing at all except a cloudless blue. There didn't seem to be the familiar shapes of New York City looming beyond them. They let in long streams of sunlight as they'd done on the clearest mornings back home, flooding the wide space with light. The information kiosk, with its ornate four-faced clock topper, which should have been in the middle of the platform, was also notoriously absent.

People seemed to be streaming in from all directions, walking in pairs or small groups. There wasn't a single person walking alone as far as I could see. Odder than that, everyone seemed to be holding the same little black book I'd been holding. It looked as if the only difference in them were that one of every pair or group had a book with gilded edges. Looking down at my companion, I saw that she had one as well, and indeed the edges of her book were gilded, too.

She seemed to catch me looking, and gave the first proper explanation in our whole interaction. "My passport's a Conductor's edition. I've made this trip a few times now. That's what those mean."

"Conductor." She nodded. I shook my head. "What's happening? None of this makes any sense. I shouldn't be here, I shouldn't be anywhere, I…"

"You're dead."

It wasn't a question. It wasn't even surprising, although it felt like this should be jarring information. On the contrary, the nerves and confusion I'd been wallowing in seemed to slip away from me with the words. It felt as if before she'd even said it, I'd figured it out, but just didn't want to admit that I knew, and suddenly there was nothing for me to do here but agree as she continued.

"Shot through the middle of the forehead."

"It was quick."

"Thankfully, yes."

I nodded. "Who's going to tell my ma? Will anyone tell her?"

The old woman just smiled again, more sadly this time, and I didn't need to ask for more than that. There were only two more questions that seemed important.

"Did I pass?"

She said handing the plain black book back to me with a smile, saying simply, "You've got a train to catch."

"Where does it go?" I took the book from her, and was strangely relieved as she patted my hand.

"Where it needs to."

She gave me another kind smile, and then there was a loud whistle, and the sounds of an engine pulling in. I looked up to see the same old black locomotive that used to pull up every morning, and realized that we'd come to the edge of the platform without me noticing. I turned to thank her, for what I wasn't sure, but she was already gone. I knew she would be.

The train puffed to a stop, and the doors opened. I joined the crowd of people thronging onto it, looking one last time over the familiar station before stepping up into the cabin and shutting the door behind me.

No, no one thinks about trying to get to Heaven. No one thinks about the logistics of it, and the rolling carousel of judges there might be waiting for you with their gilded edge books, walking with each passenger and checking their credentials before they board the train that seems to run continuously, on a perfect schedule no one knows but everyone obeys.

But honestly, people, be reasonable. There's a war on, and everyone ought to know that you always have to figure out a more efficient system to run things during rush hour.

An Apple A Day

Our supplies were running low. We had maybe a week's worth left before they came, before we were overrun and joined their putrid ranks.

Adrian had been the first one to go. Unable to bear the taste any longer, he left in the night, before anyone could stop him. When we met in the morning for our safest ritual, he was already gone, and we saw him among their number that night. One less slash through the flesh drawn from our last saving grace. One more scar on the tree's bark. One more long, pointed mask and set of bloodstained gloves.

Wes and Lex were next. They'd grown ill, and couldn't make it to the ritual, too weak to get out of bed. We knew it was too late, but we tried, damn it, we tried to protect them, just long enough. We'd have brought the ritual to them if it hadn't meant bringing the sacrifices out of the bunker, exposing them to the horde's power. Needless to say, they were gone before the sun could set.

We were picked off one by one after that. Benny, from a spot of rot that shouldn't have been there, invalidating his sacrifice. Iggy, who thought he could run to safety as the dawn broke. Tasha, when they broke through our wall and she locked the door to keep me safe.

And I am here now. And I am alone.

A week's worth for the last man standing, who would have traded it for another day with his companions at the end of the world. Now as I stare down at the fruit in my hand, the knife twisting in my other, I can't help but think of the phrase that echoes from the depths of my mind, mocking me with visions of their masked eyes and swinging lantern beams.

An apple a day keeps the doctor away.

This was my final apple, and the plague horde was closing in.

The Manor

Every town has their ghost stories, and their haunted places. Some have huge hotels with Golden Age names, full of sordid affairs and midnight rendezvous gone wrong. Some have old farm houses lost in the backcountry, steeped in the folklore of the hills and the mists of the early mornings. Some have streets you don't walk down at night for fear of what might be listening to your footsteps, and wells in the woods that you always pause to greet before moving on, but never touch.

Los Angeles is no exception, of course. There's no shortage of ghosts and specters to haunt the City of Angels, no want for dark pasts and dangerous deeds in this hotbed of Hollywood fame and infamy.

Everyone knew about the sprawling estate, with a glittering view of the ocean and a claim to one of the darkest stories in town. The Manor was infamous, and had been for decades. No one really knew what went down that October night, or in the few days that followed it. All we had to go on were a pseudo-reporter's rambling blog on Tumblr and a few short articles with fantastically gruesome headlines.

"3 Butchered in Beverly Hills Manor."

"Public Despair at the Discovery of Mayor's Mutilated Corpse."

"Unstable General Prime Suspect in Macabre Manor Murders."

Everyone had a guess. Everyone had a theory. But no one knew the truth. No one knew exactly why, on the 14th of October that year, the butler from the Manor had come running into the LAPD Headquarters, screaming about murder, and demons. What everyone did know, however, was that when the police, with sirens blaring, went to investigate the butler's wild claims, they'd been sickened to find three rotting corpses scattered around the house, in various states of dismemberment and decay.

They said the mayor's body was the worst. He looked like he'd been torn limb from limb by animals, but they never said what kind. Coyotes, people guessed, or bears, though of course that's unlikely. There was barely a bone left unbroken. They found him on the doorstep, and said it looked as if he might have fallen from the balcony on the third floor.

Then there was the body of a woman who was later identified as the wife of the manor's owner. He was an A-list actor, and she'd been his trophy piece until they separated in a messy divorce the year before. She was found in a small room on the second floor, surrounded by burned-out black candles and a bag of dry herbs and bones. She was practically perfect in appearance, they said, and they almost thought they'd found a survivor, until she crumpled under the hands of one of the officers trying to wake her. The autopsy revealed that her insides had been practically liquified.

The last body was perhaps the tamest. It was a detective who'd been reported missing a week before. He'd been shot through the right side, and left to die a slow and painful death at the top of the stairs. He was looking at the door, as if he'd watched his killer walk right out into the cool night air.

It was horrible, and it was all the media could talk about. Reporters flooded the parking lot of the station as they interviewed and interrogated the butler, but they couldn't get any sense out of him. They talked to his family and friends, but no one knew why he'd snapped. They said he'd been a perfectly sensible man in September, and now here he was, spouting nonsense about "forces beyond our control," crossing himself furiously whenever they mentioned the Manor.

What was strange was that the butler was insistent, in his rare moments of clarity, that the actor had died. He claimed to have seen him drop from the stair railings, neck broken by an unfortunate landing, and was consistent with every detail of the story no matter how many times he told it. The actor hadn't been seen since the incident, but there'd been no trace of his body when they went into the house. It was as if he'd just disappeared. Everyone assumed he'd faked it somehow, and gotten away. The manhunt lasted for years, until eventually, he was declared dead as well, another casualty of the Manor Massacre.

The Manor Massacre. The name certainly sounds good, I thought as I squinted up the dark gravel driveway. It was overgrown with weeds and bramble from years of disuse and neglect. My tires didn't like the uneven ground, and I had to pull to a stop a little earlier than I'd wanted to.

A stupid thing had led me to my dismal destination today: a dare. A simple, ridiculous dare among friends, that I wouldn't last the night in the Manor, especially on the anniversary. The fatal phrase had done me in, "You're not chicken, are you?"

I was never one to turn down a good dare. A hundred bucks was a hundred bucks, and honestly, I'd never been particularly superstitious. The worst thing I feared was the cold of this year's record-breaking October nights, and the animals that had likely taken up residence in the absence of human habitation. Stepping out of my car and shouldering my duffle bag of provisions, I surveyed the area. My first thoughts were that I wouldn't be lacking in places to camp for the night, that was certain. I trekked up the rest of the long drive, feet beginning to ache from compensating for the shifting pebbles, and up to the rusted gate, which even before I pushed it, I knew would be permanently closed and stuck. I sighed and chucked my bag over it, climbing (with much difficulty) after it and landing about as gracefully as it had.

Excellent, I thought as I rubbed my bruised knee, only another thousand yards to walk before I'm even to the door. Rich people.

The front garden was beautiful, even in its wild state. There was something to be said for the mossy stonework and the dry fountains, a kind of dystopian old-world beauty that a city-slicker like me seldom gets to see. In the city, things get rundown and turn into rubble and drug deal sites, but this place looked like the kind of ruins you'd find in old Roman cities; stunningly beautiful, in a tragic way.

Before I knew it, I was at the wide front doors, and I paused for a moment to look at the ground in front of the massive marble steps that led up to the door. There were no hints of what'd happened there, no traces left in the tall, moon-washed grass to tell me what the mayor had looked like that morning, bent and broken over them like a marionette with its strings cut. If I didn't know the stories, I wouldn't think twice about stepping through the underbrush and up the uncracked steps, which seemed to be the only things untouched by years of solitude. But I did, and my feet found their path to one side. I told myself it was out of respect for the dead.

I tested the handles, and fortune was on my side, or so I thought, as I found them unlocked. They were stiff, but I managed to swing the door open with little trouble, and stepped into the lavish front hall.

The ceiling was high, giving the hall an oversized, grand scale except that it was coated in cobwebs. The fine marble busts, mahogany side tables, and dark stone floors were covered in a layer of dust thick enough to be snow. Something moved, and I jumped before catching my reflection again in the remains of a shattered mirror, shards of which glittered on a small table below it. The sight of my own exercise-reddened face in it gave me an unexpected chill, which I chalked up to the weather hastily, and decided to move on.

I came to the main staircase, stopping at the first step to look up toward the landing. This must be the place, then, that had seen the detective's final breaths, had seen a murderer walk away to freedom and the panicked screams of a man running for his life. What had these walls seen, I wondered. If they could talk, what stories would they tell? They'd seen rich parties and scandalous affairs, carried a newlywed couple and a woman with her suitcase in the hand that should have borne a wedding band. What would they tell us about that night?

My eyes wandered into the foyer as I passed it, and I was forced to stop and double take. This time, I accepted the chill as my own reaction.

Lines of tape outlined the shape of a body in front of the fireplace, directly below the railing of the second-floor landing. This body wasn't in the right place. Officially, it didn't exist. They hadn't found a fourth body. I took a nervous step toward it. Why wouldn't they report finding this? You would think it would be important to mention to the public that they had found what looked like the detective's work on another murder. Was this where the actor had met his end, I wondered. Was this the place where the detective had found out a murderer, and decided to confront him, sealing his own fate? I suddenly found that I didn't want to know the answer.

I decided to look for a bedroom to set up in. I returned to the stairs, and climbed them by phone-flashlight, careful not to touch the railings as I went. Technically, I wasn't supposed to be here, and my footsteps were enough of a trace without leaving streaks in the dusty rails as well. As I got to the top of the stairs, my light fell on a dark stain on the wall. I slowed to a stop, staring at it. You don't need to be an expert to put two and two together and conclude that this was a blood stain. It discolored the wall in such a way that it almost looked like an outline of its own. I had a moment of silence for the fallen man, then moved quickly past his old resting place to the hall beyond, peeking in doors until I found a bedroom, just out of sight of the stairs. Perhaps I'd sleep better if I couldn't see it; I'd underestimated my own detachedness.

The room I'd entered looked as if it'd gone through hell. There were books and papers all over the floor, the musty bed was in total disarray, and a table in a little nook to my left had been violently overturned, cracking its surface and scattering a few broken picture frames on the ground. I dared to look at one of them, and found smiling back at me the same faces that'd smiled out of the articles proclaiming their deaths and disappearances.

You tended to forget in the horror of it all that before that night, the mayor, the actor, and the general had all been friends. They'd been vocally supportive of each other for years, attending each other's military events and campaign rallies and movie premiers. The photo in my hand was from the actor's wedding. He kissed his new bride, with his two closest friends clapping hands on his shoulders and smiling at him, a candid, comfortable moment during the happiest day of his life. The photo was crinkled, and the glass was missing from the frame, instead glittering around my feet.

I brought the photo with me, setting it on the side table as I dropped my bag onto the bed. It landed with a dull thud, as did I when I sat down heavily beside it. I couldn't help but feel that something was inherently wrong with this place, but I brushed that aside. I had no use for silly superstitions and fanciful interpretations of old stains and pictures. After all, this place had sat empty for going on fifty years. The killer was either long gone or long dead; I had nothing to worry about.

...

It was 2:15 AM when I squinted at my dying phone's screen, startled out of my uneasy sleep by a loud thud downstairs. "It's an animal," my brain told me lazily as my eyes hunted through the darkness of the room by the light of my screen. My heart, however, wasn't listening, and was instead trying to jump out of the frosted glass balcony doors to freedom and safety. Sighing, I stood and stretched. It looked like tonight was going to be an exploring night rather than a resting one. I pulled the real flashlight from my bag, grabbed the extra batteries and stuck them in my pocket, put my phone in there with them, on power-saving mode, and went for a walk.

I passed a small room I hadn't noticed before on the other side of the hall, and stopped to glance in the door, heart plummeting again at the sight inside.

It was little more than a closet, the only occupant of which was a small table and chair. The table was covered with a black cloth, and held candle stubs and a stack of cards, as well as a little bag. It took me a moment to connect the dots, and imagine a serenely smiling corpse with closed eyes sitting directly across from me. As I turned to leave, deciding against further exploration, I had the nagging thought that something about the room was off, other than the obvious. It wasn't until I was down the stairs again that I realized what it was. There hadn't been any dust at all in that room.

This place was definitely living up to the status of the word "manor." It seemed like an endless maze of halls and bedrooms and bathrooms and studies and media rooms and dining halls. Even the kitchen was enormous, and from its windows I could see the vast backyard that seemed more like a jungle, the green-watered swamp of a pool its oasis and the dilapidated golf course its safari plains. I wandered without thinking for the most part, trying to distract myself from the ever-lasting night with searching games. Where were the drinks stored (I didn't go down into the dark wine cellar), where were the games played (I didn't touch the royal flush still sitting on the poker table)? This worked until I found myself pushing open a door and the beam of my light fell across what I can only describe as a crime show "murder board."

Red yarn connected various fading, fragile Polaroids of a bygone age's people, some of whom I recognized from the news, some of whom were strangers to me. Yellowing articles and criminal profiles were thumb tacked to the cork boards that lined the walls. Looking a little closer, I could see that they were not the sensationalizations that I carried in my phone's picture gallery, but various stories of the lives of the victims. An old campaign poster that bore the mayor's reserved, smiling face was connected to an article about one of the actor's movies, and its failure in the box office. A front page bearing the title "Big Game Safari Hunt Gone Wrong For Ghastly General!" sat in front of a copy of a marriage certificate. Even the faces of the house's serving staff glared judgmentally back at me, with records beside them that seemed to ask me my own credentials for entering this dangerous estate.

I frowned at the handwritten notes peppering the boards, but I couldn't make heads or tails of it. The most I could get was that the actor had been in some kind of financial trouble that the mayor had been helping him with. The general had always been a bit of a wildcard, as the media had been quick to point out while pinning the murders on him, but according to these clips and scrawls, he'd been a dangerous man from the start, and it looked as if the writer was accusing him of the murder of the actor. It was strange, though; none of the confirmed murders were mentioned, and every piece here was as old as the rest of the house's furnishings. This must have been done before all the murders, I concluded, but why? Was that why the detective had been here? That was something no one had ever figured out. No one could explain his presence. Had he been hired to dig up dirt on the mayor and the general? But why? What was the actor trying to find? Or what was he hiding?

Another thud, close to me this time, shocked me out of my investigation, and as I recognized the sound of footsteps, I ducked under the heavy executive desk to hide. I was technically trespassing, though who owned this land now, I didn't know. Perhaps my friends had thought it funny to call the police and send them to pick me up, as a way of getting out of paying me. I decided that they'd pay for that later, that I'd up the bet to $150 for the inconvenience, but my main concern in the moment was staying out of sight. I held my breath as the footsteps came into the room. I didn't think about it until much, much later, when I was recounting the tale to my awestruck friends over mediocre school lunches, but from the moment I heard the first steps, a high-pitched whine droned in the background, as if some feedback from a cellphone on a cheap radio were being played constantly. It was almost like tinnitus ringing, but outside of my ears, like the sound was being sucked out of the room and pumped back in on a bad audio recording. At the time, I was more focused on not making a noise as what I assumed was a cop wandered into the room.

He stopped, pacing up and down the far end of the room, as if he were studying something on that wall. At one point, he came so close to the corner of the desk that I'd been able to see him in profile, but not being able to use my flashlight without giving myself away, I hadn't seen much other than the outline of a man in a suit, with disheveled hair that fell across the only side of his face that I could see. Then again, it was strange that I could see anything at all. The man seemed to be giving off his own light, an odd hue with a color I couldn't quite pin down, defining some of his smaller features, like the stubble of his jaw and the creases in the elbow of the otherwise immaculate suit. Perhaps he'd brought something with him to light his way, I thought, some weird lamp or flashlight. Maybe it was his phone screen. Either way, I reasoned that this man must be some kind of detective. Though why they'd sent him and not a normal beat cop, I had no idea. By this point, keeping myself from shivering was a constant, conscious effort, given that waves of wrongness seemed to radiate off of this man.

"It's quite amusing to me that you think you can hide simply by staying out of my sight and 'keeping quiet'. I must say your determination is impressive."

My heart stopped, and I couldn't tell whether I was going to shit myself or scream. I suddenly knew that I did not want this man to find me, no matter what, and that if he came over there, I wouldn't be fast enough to run. But he didn't seem to care that I was there. It sounded more like he wanted to acknowledge my presence, as if out of a want not to be rude in ignoring me.

He continued to pace, talking softly but the sound still carried. "Stay, if you like. Read all of these old lies. Make guesses, if you will. Everyone else seems to have done so already. Perhaps you'll get closer to solving the famous 'Manor Massacre.'"

I could practically hear the cold smile leave his voice then, and although it makes no sense, I would swear forever that his voice split and broke, and sounded like several people at once talking when he spoke next, covering his words with other conversations, laughter, and faint, faraway screams. "Or you could go now. Forget that you ever saw this place, and pretend it's just another mystery tale to tell your little friends while you waste your time in your silly little lives."

Suddenly, his voice was back to the soft rumble of before. "It is, of course, your choice. I suppose I'll leave you to it." His footsteps retreated back toward the door, and though I shouldn't have been able to hear it, the same soft whisper bid me goodnight.

He never said another word that I heard, and it seemed to take forever for him to actually leave. When he was finally gone, I stayed hidden for another long minute, until I was sure he'd left the house (though I ignored the fact that I'd never once heard a door open, and the footsteps had stopped at the end of the hall). I stood, shakily, flicking my flashlight on again, and froze.

There was only one set of footprints in the room, and they were the diamond-patterned prints of my own Chucks in the dust on the old wood floor.

I don't think I'd ever run faster in my life, or broken more rules of the road, than I did as I got the hell out of that place. I didn't even bother going back up to the bedroom for my bag. For all I know, it's still there.

Everyone always asks me what I think I saw. Was it a ghost? A demon? Was it the shade of the mayor, or the actor? All I can respond with is...I don't know. I don't know what I saw, or what spoke to me, or what those words meant, in the long run. And I'm certainly no closer to a positive ID of the murderer than anyone else is.

But there're certain things I never say, like how I don't think the butler was mad anymore, and how it was almost as if I could hear voices calling me as I left, the strange glow never fully dissipating as I scrambled back over the front gate and shakily started my car with the keys I'd luckily left jammed into my pocket, not even daring to turn on the headlights until I made it back off of the estate, just praying and following the gravel path back to the main road by memory and feel.

If you want a solid opinion, then here's what I think: I think I never want to know what I encountered, and that I never want to encounter it again. I think I'm going to follow his advice, and let the mystery stay unsolved. After all, it makes for a damn good story doesn't it?

Bored.

Have you ever been bored?

Most people have. Most people have experienced the kind of simple boredom that comes with the expectation that it'll be relieved by the next big event, that something will come along to change the status quo, and break you from the stupid, repetitive rut you've become trapped in.

That's not the kind of boredom I'm talking about, though.

I mean the kind of boredom that sinks into your bones and fills them with nervous energy, that crawls into the back of your mind and claws at your thoughts, breaking into your psyche like shattering glass with the thought that if you don't get out and do something, anything, anything at all, you'll go completely insane.

What if you had to live in that state constantly? What if you had to spend years alone with your thoughts, without even sight or sound or smell or touch to distract yourself from the crushing boredom of it all. What if you had to do it completely alone, in the dark and the silence, unable to move even when you so desperately want to that you strain every fiber of your being to break the bonds that hold you down, knowing deep down that you never will.

I can tell you now, it never gets easier. You never get used to it. You never do go truly insane; that'd be too much of a blessing. And I'll tell you why. Because every now and then, you'll hear something. Something very, very small, so faint that it might not be there at all except that it stands out like a flash of sunlight in the never-ending silence you're growing familiar with. An errant laugh, a faint scream, a thud or a rumble that comes from miles and miles away.

You'll focus one that sound, clinging to that small sliver of reality as it pulls you back just long enough for your scattered, broken thoughts to converge into one being once again. You'll come together just enough to think that there's a chance that you'll escape this. That they've finally found you. That they'll let you out at last and you won't have to endure another second, or minute, or hour or day or week of this suffocation without the satisfaction of nothingness at the end, this rotating wheel of torture and pain that won't even let you scream. That you'll finally be able to crawl out of hell, and rise on the other side.

Then hours will pass. You'll fight with everything in you to give some kind of sign that you're here, that you still exist. Days will pass. You'll slowly lose energy, but keep up the fight despite it all because there must be something, anything you can do. Weeks will pass. And the noise will become a faint memory, a cruel phantom of hope, taunting you just beyond your reach like the fruit of some terrible Greek myth.

And you'll be left waiting for it all to happen again, desperately wishing that they had buried your body a little bit deeper.

Six feet of earth is not enough. It's just not enough.

And I have been so bored for so long.

Abri and The Village Girl

Every day, it was the same thing. Abri watched the skinny girl stroll down the street to the bakery, and pause only for a moment to grab the bun that the man behind the counter would have ready for her almost before she appeared at the end of the road. It was always the same roll, cinnamon and clove with raisins sprinkled in, the sweet smell of it wafting down to his hiding place with an intoxicating headiness he never got tired of.

He wondered if it tasted as good as she made it look, grinning ear to ear on her way to her next stop, bits of icing crumbling into the well-trod street as she took each savored bite. When it was gone, she would be ten paces from the book shop, and the weary little shopkeep would say something kind to her.

It would always be enough to make her blush, but then again, anything would. He'd seen the way the sweet girl had hidden her face behind that striking hair that looked like a log about to burst into flame. These funny towns were filled with people colored all shades of brown, so dissimilar to his home that it made him ache for the fuller spectrum of his ancestral roads.

The girl would disappear into the store, and he would have plenty of time to dart all over town, picking up the things people had forgotten that they'd forgotten and so left to him to repurpose. He'd return, sometimes with a full stomach of lunches left unguarded and sometimes still dreaming sadly of the raisin bun, with his arms around the makings of that night's shelter, just in time to see her wave to the shopkeep before returning her arm to the still-unwavering stack of books that went from her waist to well over her head.

She'd wander down to the docks, and be there at precisely the right moment to wave at the stockyard hands as they loaded that day's departures. Then she'd sit there for hours, devouring the stack of books one after the other with a speed that left him wondering if she was really reading at all or just absorbing the materials by some kind of magic.

When the last cover snapped closed, the light would finally be fading, and she would start her slow walk back toward the end of town, stopping to bring the books back, stopping to chat with the baker, and then finally cresting the hill. And she was gone, until tomorrow, when she would return when the sun was high in the sky again.

Abri smiled to himself as she disappeared. Perhaps tomorrow, he would work up the strength to speak to her. Perhaps she would tell him her name, and he would tell her his, and they would get to be good friends. Perhaps she would teach him to read this land's strange language, and he would tell her about the sunken place the ships passed when they left her familiar harbor. She would give him that same side smile she gave the shopkeep, and he would get to pretend that it was his little Avya laughing at her brother's joke, and that he wasn't alone anymore.

Perhaps she would not mind his silver eyes or his too-light hair on too-dark skin. Perhaps she would not think he would hurt her just because he could not speak to her with as much dignity as he could in his bell-toned mother tongue, when the words of this country fell from his lips in grunts and growls. Perhaps tomorrow, this would finally come to pass, he thought as he settled into the thrown-off cotton scraps and emptied potato sacks and the light of the stars began to light the streets. Perhaps, he liked to dream. Perhaps their little routine might one day be interrupted.

The Myth of Fountains

They're all over the place: the plazas of shopping centers, the squares in small towns, at the end of garden paths and wooded walkways, in parks and places of recreation and beauty. They come in all kinds of forms, from harsh grey stone to shining silver to small wooden structures, and they're sculpted into the oddest assortment of things; they're lions or children or swirls or squares, modern or rustic or classic or natural. Fountains are amazing things, and it would be hard to deny that they were magic, at least to some degree.

Perhaps a lesser known fact about these beautiful places is this: every fountain, and indeed every body of water on the planet has a spirit of its own, if not more than one, which keeps it alive and beautiful for as long as people are willing to sacrifice even their time to enjoy it. We appear when a body comes into being and are tasked with the duties of the life source that is the water we guard, blessing the square with light and life and joyous moments since the moment we rise from the waters, and taking no greater pleasure than in hearing the laughter of those our fountains make happy.

Of the many duties we hold, one of the most famous among the world of men is our power of the wish. There is a custom, of sending us offerings of glittering coins in return for the hope of love or wealth or luck or health. This has been done for centuries and will be done for centuries hence. Most think this a myth, and do not believe in the gods of old or the spirits they pray to when they toss their offerings, but we are here, and we are listening. But there is something missing in the ritual, overzealous as mortals are in their efforts to protect the divine.

We are bound to our fountains. We cannot leave them. But you, dear ones, are free.

The Chest

"Pops?" I worried that he couldn't hear me anymore, but his head tilted toward me, the wrinkles of his forehead moving upward as a tiny smile moved over his thin lips.

With a voice like parchment, he coughed. "My dear. It is nearly time. Are you ready?"

"Pops...I have so many more questions for you. Who...who are they?"

He chuckled thinly, patting my hand without enough pressure for me to feel it if I wasn't looking. "Old friends. Old, old friends from ages ago, long before you were born."

"Friends? Pops, how are these...people, these-these *kings*...how are they your friends?"

"When I am gone..." I cringed, a tear slipping down my cheek. It was clear in his eyes as they started to wander that he couldn't see me anymore.

"When I am gone, open the chest. It will answer some of your questions. They will answer the rest." I could barely hear him anymore.

"Pops...who were you?"

"Ah, dear..." his breathing was coming slower. He struggled for a moment to gather the breath to complete his thought. "I was loved."

He didn't say another word after that.

Many hours later, I stood in front of Pops' closet.

It was too quiet in this room now, too empty after the fuss and awe of the afternoon's ceremony. I was still reeling from the attention and reverence of the highest-level people and creatures I had ever seen. They all seemed to know my name, and deferred to me. The image of a dragon bowing before me, tears shining on their scales. I stood with emperors as a pallbearer, watching kings build a pyre, and stood in the heat of dragon fire as it was set alight.

Now that it was all over, it was silent, and the mystery of my grandfather's sudden prestige loomed heavy in the air. I pushed the folding doors open, and slid a rack of old clothes aside. The smell of them was afternoon storytime by the fire, and it knocked me to my knees, freezing me to the spot. After a short eternity I shook my head, and heaved forward the big old chest that had been in the bottom of this closet for as long as I could remember.

My Pops was a kindly old man, who spoke very few words at all, and never raised his voice. He was a pushover with us kids especially, a fact that my mother never let him live down, and would let us have the run of the place as long as we were kind to it and to each other. But the one solid rule he always had was that we weren't to touch this chest. It was too dangerous, he said, but we had never been able to pry out of him what that meant.

For a second, that made me hesitate, hand hovering over the simple latch that held it closed. Who knew what would happen when I opened this box? What would scare my grandfather that badly?

I huffed a heavy sigh, and slid the latch, pushing the lid open.

Inside was...a blanket. An old, army-issue blanket, in good condition despite surely being fifty or sixty years past its prime. This didn't surprise me really, Pops had talked a few times about being a soldier many years ago, although he didn't seem to think much of that time. But this was so carefully wrapped and packed up.

I pulled the blanket up, and something fell out of it, clinking roughly against the floor.

A sword.

It was a beautifully crafted weapon, shining in the faint firelight as if it had just been set down moments ago. I didn't want to touch the blade for fear of hurting myself, but taking the hilt seemed almost as bad. It was gorgeous, a gleaming gold carved like ivy and branches and swirling down to the pommel, which held a gleaming green jewel.

Where had this come from? This wasn't a soldier's standard kit, this was...this was a prince's blade. Yes, there was the royal family's sign, etched into the stone as if it had been captured in its center like a fly in amber.

Looking back into the chest, I saw an old leather bag, and fishing it out, found it full of golden coins, some minted in a style that went out a hundred years ago. It landed with a dull thud beside the sword, and beyond it was an amulet, with the symbol of the sun god sculpted into its front. It almost seemed to be giving off its own light. Beneath that were several papers, and as I shuffled through them, careful in case they crumbled to dust beneath my fingers, and found that they were...letters? Letters, with names I'd heard all my life of people I'd only met today. Letters of recognition, letters of recommendation, contracts for work that sounded fantastical. There were dates on some of these were from a century ago.

"Who were you, old man?"

"A hero."

My head whipped around, and I saw one of the dragons, in his human form, lounging against the doorframe with his golden hair swept across his black eyes. Any other day, that would have terrified me, inspired me to bow before him and plead for his mercy. Today, I only nodded.

"Tell me. Please."

He came into the room, and sat on my grandfather's bed, patting the space beside him. I came to sit with him, letters still clasped in my hands.

"Long ago, in a different age, there were guilds of adventurers, and your grandfather led the most famous guild there was."

I shook my head. "There have been no guilds for a century."

"This is true."

"My grandfather couldn't have been..."

The dragon chuckled. "Couldn't? But why?"

"No man can live that long!"

He took one of the sheets of paper from me and skimmed through it with a rueful smile. "Can they not, now? In my time, men lived a damn sight longer than a single century. They built enormous cities dedicated to appeasing their various gods of time to keep themselves around, and yet still ran foolhardy into danger at the slightest provocation." He laughed at something he had read, and put the page down to look at me again. "I remember when your grandfather came running to my lair on just such idiotic motives."

I was still shaking my head, but it was no longer a denial. "What reason would he have had to be an adventurer? My pops didn't like trouble. He didn't even like getting up early on Sundays if he could avoid it."

"That, child, is simply old age. When you've seen the world and all the fantastic things it offers, you learn to enjoy when it offers you nothing at all."

I looked back to the sword on the ground, and the amulet beside it. "What did he do for this guild? How did he come to rule it?"

"Rule it? No. I said that he was their leader, and one only comes to lead adventurers when they have earned their respect."

"Then how did he do that?"

"By befriending those they said could never be befriended. Gods, devils, demons...dragons."

Looking back at him, the smile was still there, but sadder now. Though the eyes were black, they held the same sorrow that a grieving man's would, and the weight of a long life. I found myself reaching to touch his arm, like I would when Pops got that same, far-off look in his eyes.

"Tell me about him. I want to know who this hero was that helped raise me."

He patted my hand. He was warm to the touch, which wasn't surprising but was still disconcerting. "Then where to start? I suppose, as most of these stories do, it started with a simple quest, and a modest group of ragamuffins looking to be paid."

The Transformation

Magic doesn't feel how you would expect it to. It doesn't feel like light or wind or prayer, like something you can touch and see and control. No, magic slams into you with a force that isn't a force. It's the absence that we notice most; there is not doubling over from the sheer force of it as it happens, there is no flying backward as it hits you. Magic hits you all at once and then sinks in.

It hit him solidly in the chest, with a weight that wasn't a weight. It was almost warm, burning, searing as it seeped into his skin in an instant. When he doubled over, it wasn't from the force of it; it was in an attempt to shield himself from it, though he was far too late for that. In a sudden and intense panic, as he felt the searing that didn't hurt spread from the center of his chest out and over his body, lighting every surface on fire and setting every muscle to a smolder, he looked up at her and cried out, "Why have you done this to me? What did I do to deserve this?!"

"Why have I done this?" she repeated with disdain, "I? I have done nothing but beg and plead for your help, offer you all I have and hope that it was enough. You laughed in my face, and threw back my only payment."

His voice deepened with every word, stretched and distorted though he tried in vain to stave it off. "You-you are a stranger! A stranger, who...who comes to my home and demands, with no preface and no invitation, demands my respect, my hospitality-!"

"I AM WHAT YOU FEAR!" she bellowed as he cowered, as he watched the ground slide away from him though his feet remained planted. "I AM ONE WHO BEGS ALL AND RETURNS IT MORE THAN IN FULL FOR THE SMALL COST OF YOUR TIME WHEN TIME IS ALL YOU HAVE TO GIVE."

He grew heavier and heavier, sinking to his knees with an unfamiliar weight, and itched as if his skin were covered in crawling bugs.

"Then my time I will take back. Ten years you would have had of prosperity and growth, blessings beyond your imaginings. Ten years, your gates would have always opened upon full orchards and fields overflowing, and your ballroom would have been light with laughter and music to rival Heaven. So, ten years, you will be silent, and your gates will be frozen as your heart, and no human comfort will you find. Ten years, your home will be forgotten and you, alone, will bear the weight. Your servants will join you, but still, there will be no human comfort. They will be as you see them."

A scream echoed in the hall; the servants began to flee in terror, but she held them in place with the barest glance. His hands, if hands they still were, slammed into the cobbles. He had not realized the steps were behind him now, and he craned his unbalanced head to see lights coming on in every window, shapes scrambling for the castle walls, and being thrown back with violent flashes of light. Slowly, the shapes were disappearing, but the noise did not abate. It was deafening. He turned back to the woman, the terror setting into his heart.

"You...would curse them, as well? Would make them suffer for my supposed sins?"

"They will not suffer. Whatever your outcome, they will survive. They will fade from this place, without memory of you or your home. They will be here only as long as they are remembered, will forget as forgotten. But they will not know this. And you will not know this."

And as it was said, it left his memory.

"For their part, they will be to you as they have always been. Unseen. Silent. Only there to do your will. They will have only each other for company."

He realized what this meant as a scullery maid ran before him, hands vanishing before here already ethereal face. No longer able to bear his own weight, he collapsed with a snarl fitting to what he might be becoming. It was all he could do to stare up at her as his vision faded.

"I will send hope for you. Another will come here, and you will have again the opportunity to offer shelter. If you can earn the honest love of another, the curse will be broken. If not, you will remain outwardly what you are inwardly...a beast."

The darkness consumed him.

The Screams

The first thing that it...he?...remembered was screaming.

The sound, for that was what he found it was called much later, seemed to hit him physically, so that, if he could have moved his arms yet, he would have clawed at his ears, trying desperately to pull out the painful spikes that drilled into his skull. As it was, he remembered instinctively struggling away from them, feeling the cold of the table shift beneath him, shortly realizing that this motion was his and thereby finding that he was able to stand.

The screaming continued unyielding as he became aware of his other senses. He began to feel the pain of his stiff and atrophied muscles, pulling over unfamiliar bones and under skin that did not sit right on them. He smelled the stiff, chemical smell of the room, known to be unnatural even to one who did not know what nature was. This sharp scent caused him to gasp, a startled, stuttering breath that became a scraping groan of discomfort. It repelled him, causing him to stumble backward.

Through it all, the screaming continued, and as he discovered how to, he turned to see what was making the noise. His eyes met with those of another creature, one he would come to know as a man. This man's face was contorted with the effort of the screams, eyes wide. This spectre with its gaping mouth, though unsettling, was the only other thing that seemed to move, to have any sort of agency over this overwhelming world. Though he had no words, his throat croaked again, and groaned to call out to this one hope for his saving.

This sent the man scrambling backward, and he, not knowing what else to do, stumbled forward again. The man before him turned on his heel and, with the effortless movements of one acquainted with this world, bolted through the door on the far end of the room, slamming it sharply behind him. The room was suddenly silent, and he found himself utterly alone. For some reason, this was more unsettling than the screaming.

It was moments later that he smelled the acrid odor he would learn meant smoke. Smoke, which led to flame, and this meant more agony. Soon he would learn what it meant to scream, and, crouching now in the walls of the family's home, the creature, as he'd come to call himself after the fashion of his creator, would come to know that screaming would be all he was destined to cause in this world he'd been forced back into.

Based on Mary Shelley's Frankenstein.

Author's Note

On the next few pages, you'll find another beginning. This one, however, is already well on its way to becoming a middle, and possibly an ending as well. What you're about to read is a portion of the first chapter of my next novel, a sci-fi horror story provisionally titled *Oasis 8*. It was created as my NaNoWriMo2020 project. This is a very early draft, so of course it will not look the same in the final version of the book, but I am more than excited to share it with you in its current form.

I'm not sure when it will be published, but rest assured, I'm as excited as you are.

Enjoy!

Cat

It Shouldn't Have Been Empty

Pulling into Oasis 8 should have been a pain in the ass.

People liked to compare it to stopping at a truck stop off of I-75, near as dammit to Atlanta. You don't want to do it during peak times because you'll never get out without a fender bender. Problem is, there are no off-peak times. It's always busy, always crowded, always annoying to try and navigate your way through the waves of ships as they cruise around, vaguely following interstellar traffic law if you squinted hard enough. There was always a loud-mouthed asshole with a supped-up ship made from scrap parts you'd have to skirt around to avoid a messy, aggressive confrontation that usually ended with one or both of you in Oasis 8's holding cells, waiting on Council reprimands or jail time.

That's what we were expecting, and what we'd been preparing for for the past month; we knew we were going to have to stop to refuel before we got to the outer ring. Hell, everyone does, you can't make it that far even with high-end high-efficiency tanks, and there's only one place to park it before you hit the dead zone. Eight was the biggest international space station to date, equipped with enough ports to temporarily house up to thirty commercially sized cruisers and enough interior space for 1500 people to sleep in relative comfort for upwards of twenty days. Really, that many people weren't meant to exist in such a small place together for so long, so tensions were always high and people were always rude.

To make it worse, the traffic was the worst anywhere in the system, and that's without having backseat drivers on the comms filtering the rude commentary and getting just as fed up with it as you are, telling you to "just dock the damn thing, already." Oh yeah? You try piloting a cruiser into a port with needle precision while twenty others try to do the same thing all around you, spitting criticisms of everything from your approach technique to your gender, and then tell me if you can "just dock it."

But today was strange.

"Is it just me or...or is it really not busy today?"

Jared's voice rang out in the uncomfortable silence as we all watched our ship glide toward the silent, still station. Only our ship. We were the only ones pulling into port, and it wasn't sitting well with anyone.

I frowned over at him for a moment before returning to docking procedures. "Maybe we hit it in the off season." I'd tried for nonchalance, but it sounded false even to me.

"They don't have an off season," he muttered under his breath, but we heard him. He let it go, tapping away at his navigation screen and the com deck, fiddling with dials and buttons and swiping through screens as he tried to connect.

"Endeavor 101 to Oasis 8, permission to dock in station five?"

Static and silence.

"Endeavor 101 to Oasis 8, do you copy?"

"Are you connected?"

"Uh," he checked the line again, and his frown deepened. "No. No, I'm not getting through at all."

"Is something blocking it? Do they have shields up for some reason?" Audrey asked, leaning over Jared's shoulder. She'd come up from her navigation setup, and the book she'd been pretending unsuccessfully to read. Her eyes flicked between Jared's screens and the window panels. "Like, are we too far from the station still?"

"No, of course we're not, we're in docking distance," I said sharply, adjusting our trajectory. We were driving closer, but I hadn't actively pulled in yet. I didn't want to arrive unannounced, but something in my gut was also warning me to stay back. "We should have been able to reach them half an hour ago."

"I thought the lines were busy," Jared said, checking his connection and refreshing it again. "That's happened before, usually it isn't a big deal."

"The lines might be down? Maybe they're doing maintenance?" No one seemed to believe this, not even Audrey, who couldn't help but look worried even as she said it. Her eyes were still focused out on the station, and in the emptiness surrounding it. "Is it just me, or does it just look really...still?"

Jared tried again, fiddling with his settings. "Oasis 8, do you read? Hello? Anyone on?"

Audrey tore her eyes away from the shields and looked back at me. "What're you thinking, Cap?"

I was really hoping neither of them would ask me that. "I'm thinking...that Jared should shoot a message back to control if he can. Tell them what we see."

"On it."

Jared's attention was absorbed into the screen again, so he didn't see Audrey come up beside me and crouch closer to the jump seat. We both looked out at the silent station, searching for a sign of...anything.

"Maybe there was a structural problem, and they had to evacuate?"

The station was the most advanced structure ever made. It'd gone through rigorous testing for years before anyone was allowed to set foot in there without a suit and a tether, and there were safeguards upon safeguards for hull breaches and airlock failures. Even if something catastrophic had happened, it shouldn't have caused an evacuation; it should have just caused that section of the station to be closed off for repairs. Oasis 8 could, and had, run on half its space and a quarter of its power if it needed to. To have something big enough to shut it all down would have been on the front page of every news outlet from here to the system edge.

Still, I nodded slightly. "If that's the case, we should check in and see if there are any stragglers. We may have to write up a report. Jared."

He looked up at his name, brows still furrowed low in concern. "Ask if they've gotten any reports back."

"Yep."

I focused back in on guiding us into the dock. Without the usual kerfuffle, it was almost too easy, and as the ship was caught by the landing gears and holding fields, as the fuel line slid out and connected, ready to start refueling, I thought about the last time I'd been through. New behind the wheel of a small training ship. It'd been the first time I'd gone totally off-planet, not just skirting around the moon and back. Most pilots have their "graduation" trip to Oasis 8; it's a good way to network with other sailors and build a crew of your own. I'd actually met Jared here, in the third floor cantina where we'd both been taking our leave time to grab a drink. He was from one of the midway colonies, and hadn't met an Earth kid before, so we talked all night, commiserating about growing up in the inner rings and dreaming about getting to see the edges of the solar system and beyond. We'd parted ways that night, but kept in touch, and a year later when I was hired on as a freight driver, he was the first person I'd called.

As docking was finalized, Jared spoke up, pulling me out of my reminiscing. "So I got in touch with ground control."

"What'd they say?" Audrey was pulling up the spacewalk suits.

"They hadn't gotten any reports. Said Eight had been dark for a few days."

Audrey and I stopped in our tracks and stared.

"Days?" I repeated. "And they didn't send a crew?"

"They'd been told not to."

"Why would they have been told not to?" Audrey asked, looking as shaken as I felt. Jared shrugged, but he didn't say anything else. There was a long moment of uncomfortable silence.

"Well. Looks like we will be putting in that report," I said, walking to the suits and grabbing mine. "Come on. Let's go take a look."

We went through our usual checks to see if the air was holding steady outside, and if it'd be safe for us to go without suits. Even when the readings came back normal on our ship, we waited until we were out and double checked the readings to take off our helmets.

Even the loading dock screamed of something wrong. There was no loud crew there, jostling around to do maintenance on the ship or double check the fuel line or annoy us with customs questions. Audrey checked the line and started the autofueler, while Jared and I walked around the dock to see if there was anyone around. It was uncomfortably quiet, and our shouts of "Hello? Is anyone here?" rang off the walls unnaturally loudly. We came back to the landing gate and looked toward the hall to the main atrium.

"We should go back," Audrey said. She was calm, but it was clear that this wasn't sitting well with her. Hell, it wasn't sitting well with any of us. Jared put a gloved hand on her shoulder, but she shrugged him off. "Clearly there's no one here, and we're not qualified to deal with emergencies like this."

"I know," I said, nodding, "and I agree. I don't want to be here any more than you do. It doesn't feel right."

"So what, we just camp in the ship until it's done refueling, then turn around?" Jared seemed to like the idea, but I sighed heavily.

"No. We need to get some kind of read on what happened so we can go back and tell them." The others shifted uncomfortably. I knew they'd do whatever I asked them to, and I didn't like having to put them in this kind of situation, but it was a necessary evil.

"Listen, we've got what, two hours before the ship is fully fueled?" They nodded. "So we take a look around, see if we can find anyone or any clue as to what happened, and when two hours is up, we leave. Okay?"

They looked at me, then at each other. Then Jared nodded.

"Two hours."

Audrey's shoulders fell a bit, resigned. "Two hours."

"Two hours," I agreed, and turned back to the main hall.

It was strange walking into the concourse and not finding anyone running around. The soaring ceiling and circular room made it feel like the place should be full of constant motion. Designed after all of our sci-fi stories, even after we'd already had the tech for years, this place felt straight out of a classic space movie, like something from the far off future, a hub of chatter and laughter and constant energy that meant everyone was working together to go further out than ever before. To not have that...well, it felt wrong.

As we fanned out into the main room, I looked out over the café tables that lined the little food court in this area. There were a few that'd been knocked over, as if there'd been a rauchus fight. Some of them still had plates of half-eaten food on them. They must have gotten up in a hurry, I thought.

I tripped on something and heard it clink away. I turned to look at it. It was a little coffee mug. Why had it been lying in the middle of the floor? It was like someone was going to walk through this empty, scruffed up doorway and pick it up, complaining to their buddy that "So-and-so never puts their mugs up when they're done!" They'd probably talk about how So-and-so could never finish one cup of coffee before it went cold, and then they'd have to make themselves a new one.

Somehow, it wasn't comforting to think of the silly little conversation that might have been, considering the cup was just sitting there, with its chipped rim and pink lipstick stains, and the dredge of long-dried coffee at the very bottom, one last sip that went cold too soon.

I picked it up to show to the others, but Jared called out. "Hey, guys?"

Looking over, I saw him pointing down the hall that led to one of the loading bays. The sign on the wall had been knocked askew, the "Bay 15" scraped down the middle. It was unsettling, but it wasn't what he was pointing at. His finger was directed at the floor some ten feet down the hall. "What's that?"

Audrey and I joined him, and looked at the dark stain. I took the lead, walking in to get a closer look, and found that there were more stains. They continued down the hall, seemingly at random. Some were on the floor, some on the walls, one or two spray patterns across the ceiling.

Not only that, the hall looked like it'd been hit by a tornado. Pieces of torn apart chairs were scattered across the floor, the little decorative plants and end tables knocked over with dirt scattering all over the ground and leaves torn to shreds. The pictures that'd been on the wall were tilted at slightly sickening angles, some having fallen off completely, and nearly all of them were missing their glass covering entirely, glittering shards of it littering the hallway.

I bent down beside the stain to get a better look at it. The ground in here was carpeted in a dark slate grey, an industrial color that made it hard to tell anything about the stain other than the fact that it was very dark, and oddly big.

"Looks like something spilled and never got cleaned up. Coffee? Or oil, maybe?" But it was too big to be a coffee stain, and there was no reason to bring oil this far into the concourse.

"Here, hang on, let me get some light on it." Jared swung a flashlight off of his hip and turned it on, aiming at the stain. In the stark white circle of it, the stain took on a much different appearance.

I reeled back slightly.

"What?" Audrey said, leaning over Jared's shoulder.

I was still staring at the stain.

When I was a kid, I'd broken my arm pretty badly. I was running around our house with my brother, and I'd somehow ended up falling down the stairs. I'd gashed my arm and split the bone, so when I hit the carpet in our living room, I'd been gushing. I got taken to the hospital and patched up pretty quickly, but it'd taken my mother a week to really scrub it clean. It was the first time I'd seen something like that, and that kind of thing sticks.

So seeing this stain, the pattern of it finally clicking, the dark color finally lit up by the light, I recognized it instantly.

"Blood," I said quietly. I looked up from the stain on the floor to the others. In patches all down the floor. On the walls. A few sprays on the ceiling.

"It's all blood."

They both took a step back, eyes finding the rest of the stains just as quickly as I had.

"We should go," Audrey said, voice quivering, "Oh my god, we should go."

"Jesus," Jared breathed. He swung the flashlight around the hall. "That's so much...what happened?"

"I don't think whoever made these stains made it out," I said bluntly. Audrey cringed, but Jared nodded. We'd all begun retreating toward our ship. "I think you might have been on the right track about us staying on the ship, Jared."

"Yeah," he said, with obvious relief, "We should go..." He trailed off, face frozen for a second on a relieved smile that quickly dropped into a frown. His eyes were fixed on the end of the hall.

"What's up?"

"I...did you see that?" He gestured, and we looked but I couldn't see anything. "It was right there, something moved." He took a step forward. "Hello?"

His voice echoed down the hall, but there was no response.

Audrey put a hand on his shoulder. "Come on. Let's go."

He seemed reluctant, but he followed her. His eyes kept darting back over our shoulders. "I could have sworn I saw..."

"Was it a person?" I asked, looking back as well.

"I don't think so?" His frown was fixed. "It was fast. I only saw the shadow, I think, and they must have been crouched or something because it looked weird."

"Maybe it was a pet or something?"

"Maybe."

None of us were convinced. Without discussing it, we all walked a little faster back toward the ship.

About the Author

Cat Webling is an actress and author based in middle Georgia. She started writing professionally in 2018, when she published her first novel, *Artificial Intelligence*. She continues to write from her home, which she shares with her mom, dad, little brother, and lovely dog.

If you enjoy her work, you can find her here:

The Bookshelf at www.catwebling.com[1] | @catwebling on Medium.com | @CatWebling on Twitter | @catwebling on Instagram | Cat Webling on Facebook | KittyCatThang on YouTube

---

1. http://www.catwebling.com

Also by Cat Webling

Artificial Intelligence
Fruits and Finery
The Fading of the Day
The Clockwork Figurine
Ghost
The Symmetry of Falling Leaves
Between Spaces
For I Am Fearless

Watch for more at https://www.catwebling.com/.